Addiction

Too close to home

Brenda A. Gaier

First Edition

Dedication

This book is dedicated to my husband, Jim, whose love, strength, and steady presence carried me through some of the most difficult moments of our lives. Your patience, understanding, and unwavering support gave me the courage to tell this story honestly and with heart. Through the challenges, the long nights, and the emotional weight of these experiences, you never stopped believing in me. This book exists because of you, and it is written with deep gratitude and love.

Acknowledgement

I am deeply thankful to my wonderful husband, Jim, for reading early drafts of this book and offering his thoughtful advice. Without his support, this book would not have been possible. I am also grateful to my mother for her unwavering love and for always being there for me.

I would like to thank our children for their help with research and for their continued support throughout this journey.

My sincere appreciation goes to my publisher, Mark Wilson, for guiding me patiently through the publishing process. And of course, a special thank you to our dog, Kia, for keeping me company during the many hours of writing.

Table of Contents

CHAPTER 1

UNDERSTANDING ADDICTION

IN CHILDREN

The Nature of Addiction

For parents of children with substance problems, understanding the nature of addiction is crucial. It involves a blend of biological, psychological, and environmental factors that can influence a child's behavior and choices. Recognizing that addiction is a disease rather than a moral failing can help parents approach the situation with empathy rather than judgment, paving the way for more effective communication and support.

My personal experience with two of my own children, when they were late teens and early adults, was that we went through the most terrifying situations as parents that we have ever had to deal with. There was stealing, manipulation, rage, fights, dealing with the police, arrests, jail, court, probation, and a lot more.

 My kids would look you dead in the eye and lie to you, and you would believe every word, because you love them and cannot believe that your child would ever lie to you. They would beg for money using some excuse as to why they need it. We would get calls from some jail in the middle of the night, and they would want us to bail them out and tell us they would never do it again. When they are using, they don't care about you or anything else; they are just chasing that next high.

After all the things we went through as parents, we became kind of numb. You want so badly to believe everything they tell you, but you can't. Eventually, we got to the point that we realized what we were doing was enabling them. We thought it was love; they thought it was them getting one over on you. We had to take the hard road and just say NO. This went on for not just a short time; I'm talking years. The sleepless nights, not knowing where they were, going for car rides to look for them, and wondering if they are alright.

In 2023, there were 708 deaths from overdose in children between the ages of 13 and 17. Overdoses are the third leading cause of adolescent deaths. The majority of these deaths are because of synthetic opioids, primarily fentanyl, often found in counterfeit pills. This number is twice the pre-pandemic figure of 282 deaths in 2019.

Different types of addiction manifest in children, ranging from alcohol and drug abuse to behavioral addictions like gaming or gambling. Each type carries its own set of challenges and requires tailored strategies for intervention. Parents must educate themselves about these various forms of addiction to effectively recognize signs in their children. Learning to differentiate between normal adolescent behavior and concerning patterns of use that may warrant professional help.

Open communication is paramount when addressing addiction. Parents should strive to create an environment where their children feel safe discussing their struggles without fear of punishment or shame. This means actively listening to their child's concerns and feelings while maintaining a non-confrontational stance. Engaging in conversations about addiction can be difficult, but using supportive language and expressing love can encourage children to be more honest about their experiences and challenges.

Seeking professional help is often necessary for children facing addiction. This can include locating therapists who specialize in adolescent substance abuse, as well as identifying support groups for both children and parents. These resources can provide invaluable guidance and coping strategies, helping families navigate the complexities of addiction. Parents should not hesitate to reach out for help, as many have faced similar challenges and can offer insights based on their experiences.

Creating a supportive home environment is essential for recovery. This involves establishing clear rules and expectations while also fostering a culture of healthy habits within the family. Engaging in family activities that promote wellness, such as exercising together or preparing nutritious meals, can strengthen family bonds and provide a positive distraction from substance use. Additionally, parents must take care of their mental health, ensuring they have their own support networks to lean on during this challenging time, thereby maintaining resilience for both themselves and their children.

Signs and Symptoms of Addiction

Recognizing the signs and symptoms of addiction in children is crucial for parents who want to help their loved ones. Often, these signs may manifest as changes in behavior, mood swings, or physical health issues. Parents may notice their child becoming increasingly secretive or isolating themselves from family and friends, which can raise red flags about potential substance use. Understanding these behavioral shifts is the first step in addressing the problem and seeking appropriate help.

Another common symptom of addiction is a decline in academic performance. Children who are struggling with substance abuse may lose interest in school, leading to falling grades and absenteeism. It's essential for parents to monitor their child's academic engagement and social interactions, as these can provide significant clues about their well-being. Open discussions about school and friends can help parents gauge their child's state and encourage healthier coping strategies.

Physical symptoms also play a significant role in identifying addiction. Parents might observe changes in their child's appearance, such as weight loss or neglect of personal hygiene. Additionally, frequent nosebleeds, bloodshot eyes, or unusual smells may indicate substance use. Being vigilant about these physical changes can prompt vital conversations about health and the risks associated with substance abuse.

Emotional symptoms are equally important to consider. Children dealing with addiction may exhibit signs of anxiety, depression, or irritability. They might also experience mood swings that can affect their relationships with family members and peers. Parents should be aware of these emotional indicators and seek to create a supportive environment where their child feels safe discussing their feelings openly. This can lead to more effective communication and a better understanding of their child's struggles.

Ultimately, recognizing the signs and symptoms of addiction requires awareness, empathy, and action from parents. By understanding these indicators, parents can take proactive steps to seek professional help, engage in meaningful conversations, and foster a supportive home environment. This approach not only aids in addressing their child's addiction but also promotes overall family well-being and resilience during challenging times.

Different Types of Substances Commonly Abused

Substance abuse among children can manifest through various types of substances, each with its own risks and effects. Commonly abused substances include alcohol, nicotine, vapes, marijuana, prescription medications, and illicit drugs like cocaine, heroin, fentanyl, and meth. Understanding these substances is crucial for parents to recognize the signs of addiction and to intervene effectively. Awareness of what these substances are, how they are used, and their potential impacts on health and behavior can empower parents in their efforts to support their children through recovery.

CHAPTER 2

COPING WITH YOUR CHILD

Acknowledging Your Feelings

Acknowledging your feelings is a crucial first step for parents dealing with a child's substance abuse. It's essential to recognize and validate your emotions, whether it's fear, anger, guilt, or sadness. These feelings are natural responses to a challenging situation, and understanding them can help you navigate the complex landscape of addiction and recovery. By acknowledging your feelings, you can begin to process them productively rather than letting them overwhelm you.

You may find yourself oscillating between hope and despair, especially when your child's behavior fluctuates. This emotional rollercoaster can leave you feeling isolated and confused. It's important to connect with others who understand your situation, such as support groups or therapists. Sharing your experiences can provide comfort and clarity, reminding you that you're not alone in this journey.

As you confront your feelings, consider how they impact your interactions with your child. Your emotional state can influence your communication, making it either supportive or confrontational. When discussing addiction, try to approach conversations with empathy and an open mind. This fosters an environment where your child feels safe to express themselves, increasing the likelihood of productive dialogue about their struggles.

In addition to communication, managing your feelings is vital for maintaining your mental health. Engage in self-care practices that help you cope with stress, such as exercise, mindfulness, or hobbies. These activities can provide a necessary outlet, allowing you to recharge and approach your child's addiction with a clearer perspective. Remember, taking care of yourself is not selfish; it's essential for being an effective support system for your child.

Acknowledging Your Feelings

Acknowledging your feelings is a crucial first step for parents dealing with a child's substance abuse. It's essential to recognize and validate your emotions, whether it's fear, anger, guilt, or sadness. These feelings are natural responses to a challenging situation, and understanding them can help you navigate the complex landscape of addiction and recovery. By acknowledging your feelings, you can begin to process them productively rather than letting them overwhelm you.

You may find yourself oscillating between hope and despair, especially when your child's behavior fluctuates. This emotional rollercoaster can leave you feeling isolated and confused. It's important to connect with others who understand your situation, such as support groups or therapists. Sharing your experiences can provide comfort and clarity, reminding you that you're not alone in this journey.

As you confront your feelings, consider how they impact your interactions with your child. Your emotional state can influence your communication, making it either supportive or confrontational. When discussing addiction, try to approach conversations with empathy and an open mind. This fosters an environment where your child feels safe to express themselves, increasing the likelihood of productive dialogue about their struggles.

In addition to communication, managing your feelings is vital for maintaining your mental health. Engage in self-care practices that help you cope with stress, such as exercise, mindfulness, or hobbies. These activities can provide a necessary outlet, allowing you to recharge and approach your child's addiction with a clearer perspective. Remember, taking care of yourself is not selfish; it's essential for being an effective support system for your child.

Ultimately, acknowledging your feelings is about creating a foundation for healing and recovery within your family. By recognizing your emotions and seeking help when needed, you set a positive example for your child. This journey may be difficult, but with the right tools and support, you can foster an environment that encourages both you and your child to thrive in the face of adversity.

Understanding the Impact on Family Dynamics

Family dynamics can be profoundly affected when a child struggles with substance abuse. Parents may experience a whirlwind of emotions, including confusion, anger, sadness, and helplessness. These feelings can create tension within the household, often leading to misunderstandings and conflicts among family members. Understanding how addiction alters family interactions is crucial for parents seeking to regain harmony and support their child's recovery journey.

Communication becomes a key challenge in families dealing with addiction. Parents might find it difficult to talk openly about their child's substance use, fearing rejection or confrontation. However, fostering an environment where open dialogue is encouraged can significantly improve relationships. By actively listening and expressing concern without judgment, parents can help their children feel safe to share their struggles and experiences, thereby strengthening family bonds.

Seeking professional help is often necessary to navigate the complexities of addiction. Therapists and support groups can offer invaluable resources and strategies for families. Parents should not hesitate to reach out for help, as this not only supports their child's recovery but also aids in their own emotional well-being. Finding local support networks or engaging in family therapy can empower families to address the issues collaboratively and constructively.

Creating a supportive home environment is essential for recovery. This involves establishing routines, setting clear boundaries, and promoting healthy habits within the family. Engaging in family activities that foster connection, such as cooking together or participating in outdoor activities, can enhance relationships and provide children with positive alternatives to substance use. Parents should prioritize nurturing a home where love, support, and understanding are foundational values.

Lastly, maintaining mental health is vital for parents facing these challenges. Coping mechanisms, such as mindfulness practices, exercise, and connecting with other parents in similar situations, can provide much-needed relief. By taking care of their own well-being, parents are better equipped to support their child through recovery. Understanding the impact of addiction on family dynamics allows parents to take proactive steps toward healing and rebuilding their family life together.

Setting Realistic Expectations

Setting realistic expectations is crucial for parents navigating the challenging landscape of their child's substance abuse. Understanding that recovery is not a linear process can help alleviate feelings of frustration and disappointment. Many parents hope for immediate results, but it is vital to recognize that healing takes time, patience, and consistent effort. This journey may involve setbacks, and acknowledging this reality can foster a more supportive environment for both the parent and the child.

Parents should also remember that each child's experience with addiction is unique. Factors such as the type of substance used, the duration of use, and individual psychological profiles all play significant roles in recovery. By focusing on your child's specific situation, you can set more personalized and attainable goals. This can lead to a greater sense of accomplishment as you celebrate small victories along the way, reinforcing positive behaviors and encouraging ongoing progress.

Communication with your child about their addiction is another area where realistic expectations are essential. Parents often wish to have open and honest conversations, but it is important to approach these discussions with empathy and understanding. Expecting your child to immediately accept their situation or respond positively to conversations may not always be realistic. Instead, prepare for a gradual process where trust is built over time, allowing your child to feel safe sharing their feelings and experiences.

Seeking professional help is a vital step in addressing addiction, and parents should maintain an open mind about the different types of treatment available. Understanding that therapy, support groups, and rehabilitation programs vary in their approach can help set realistic expectations regarding outcomes. By actively participating in your child's recovery journey and being open to various treatment modalities, you can better navigate the complexities of recovery and contribute positively to their healing process.

Finally, creating a supportive home environment is essential for fostering recovery. Parents should focus on establishing routines, healthy communication patterns, and engaging in family activities that promote well-being. However, it is crucial to recognize that perfection is not attainable, and mistakes will happen along the way. Emphasizing a culture of support, love, and understanding within the home will ultimately lead to a more conducive atmosphere for your child's recovery journey.

CHAPTER 3

STRATEGIES FOR COMMUNICATING WITH YOUR CHILD ABOUT ADDICTION

Choosing the Right Time and Place

Choosing the right time and place to discuss your child's substance abuse is crucial for fostering open communication. It's important to find a setting where both you and your child feel comfortable and safe. A calm and private environment allows for honest dialogue without distractions or interruptions. Consider their state of mind and your own, ensuring that emotions are manageable before initiating this significant conversation.

Timing also plays a vital role in these discussions. Avoid bringing up the topic during moments of heightened emotion or conflict, such as after an argument or when your child is under stress. Instead, look for moments of calm, perhaps during a shared activity or when you are both relaxed at home. This approach can help create a more conducive atmosphere for dialogue, where your child is more likely to be receptive.

Additionally, think about the emotional readiness of your child. If they are currently in crisis or using substances, it may be best to wait until they are in a more stable state. Preparing for this conversation involves not only choosing the right moment but also being equipped with knowledge about addiction and recovery options. This preparation will enable you to provide supportive guidance and information in a way that resonates with your child's experience.

It may also be beneficial to include other family members in these discussions. Family support can reinforce the message that recovery is a collective effort and that everyone is invested in your child's well-being.

Creating a family meeting to discuss addiction and recovery can strengthen bonds and foster a sense of unity as you navigate this challenging journey together.

Ultimately, the goal of choosing the right time and place is to create an open channel of communication that encourages your child to share their feelings and struggles. This approach not only enhances understanding but also builds a foundation of trust, which is essential for effective recovery. By being intentional about when and where you discuss these topics, you are taking proactive steps toward supporting your child's journey to recovery.

Active Listening Techniques

Active listening is an essential skill for parents dealing with children who have substance abuse issues. It involves fully focusing, understanding, responding, and remembering what the other person is communicating. By practicing active listening, parents can create a safe space for their children to express their feelings and thoughts about their addiction. This approach not only fosters trust but also encourages open dialogue, which is crucial for navigating the complexities of addiction.

One effective technique is to give your child your undivided attention. This means putting away distractions such as phones or television when having a conversation. By maintaining eye contact and using affirming nods, parents can show their children that they are truly engaged. This level of attentiveness can help children feel valued and understood, making them more likely to share their struggles and triumphs with their parents.

Another important aspect of active listening is to practice reflective listening. This technique involves paraphrasing or summarizing what your child has said to ensure that you have understood their message correctly. For example, if your child expresses frustration about school pressures and substance use, a parent might respond with, "It sounds like you're feeling overwhelmed by everything that's going on at school, and it's affecting your choices." This not only clarifies the child's feelings but also shows that the parent is genuinely trying to understand their perspective.

Additionally, parents should avoid jumping to conclusions or offering immediate advice when their child is speaking. Instead, they should allow their child to finish their thoughts fully before responding. This can help to prevent misunderstandings and make the child feel heard. By creating an atmosphere where children can freely discuss their feelings, parents can better understand the underlying issues contributing to their addiction.

Finally, practicing patience is key in active listening. Conversations about addiction can be emotional and challenging, and it may take time for children to articulate their feelings. Parents should be prepared for moments of silence and be comfortable sitting with their child's discomfort. By demonstrating patience and empathy, parents can reinforce their support, making it clear that they are there for their child throughout their recovery journey.

Approaching Difficult Conversations

Approaching difficult conversations with your child about substance abuse can be one of the most challenging aspects of parenting. It is crucial to create a safe space for dialogue, where your child feels heard and understood. Start by choosing a calm, private setting, free from distractions, to ensure that both you and your child can engage openly. Expressing your concern should come from a place of love rather than judgment. This approach fosters trust and encourages your child to share their feelings and experiences without fear of retribution.

Listening actively is a vital part of these conversations. It is essential to allow your child to express their thoughts and emotions fully. Avoid interrupting or jumping to conclusions, as this can shut down communication and create defensiveness. Validate their feelings, even if you don't fully understand their perspective. This demonstrates empathy and respect for their experience, which can lead to more productive discussions about their struggles with addiction.

It's also important to be prepared for resistance or denial during these conversations. Children dealing with addiction may not be ready to acknowledge their issues, and they might react with anger or withdrawal.

Stay calm and patient, reiterating your love and support. Reassure them that your goal is to help, not to punish. If the conversation becomes too heated, it might be beneficial to take a break and revisit the topic later when emotions have cooled.

Setting clear expectations and boundaries is necessary after these discussions. Let your child know what behaviors are unacceptable and the consequences of continued substance use. However, it's crucial to balance this with a supportive environment where recovery is encouraged. Offer resources, such as therapy or support groups, to help them navigate their addiction. Showing that you are willing to seek help together can empower your child and reinforce the importance of recovery.

Finally, remember to take care of yourself during this process. Parenting a child with substance abuse issues is emotionally taxing, and it's vital to maintain your mental health. Engage in self-care activities, seek support from friends or groups, and consider professional help if needed. By prioritizing your well-being, you will be in a better position to support your child through their recovery journey.

CHAPTER 4

SEEKING PROFESSIONAL HELP

Identifying the Right Type of Therapist

Finding the right type of therapist for your child can be a daunting task, especially when faced with the challenges of substance abuse. It's essential to understand that different therapists specialize in various areas, including addiction, trauma, and mental health. Start by identifying your child's specific needs and the type of support they require. This initial understanding will guide you in selecting a professional who is well-equipped to help your child navigate their recovery journey.

When considering therapists, look for credentials and experience in treating substance abuse among adolescents. Some therapists may focus on behavioral therapies, while others might integrate family therapy or holistic approaches. Researching potential therapists' backgrounds and methodologies can provide valuable insight into how they may resonate with your child. Don't hesitate to ask about their experience with similar cases and their approach to fostering recovery in young individuals.

It is also vital to consider the therapeutic setting that will best suit your child. Some kids may thrive in a one-on-one environment, while others might benefit from group therapy, where they can connect with peers facing similar challenges. Understanding your child's personality and comfort level can significantly influence their willingness to engage in therapy. Discussing these options with them can empower them in their recovery process.

Moreover, the therapeutic relationship is crucial for successful outcomes. A therapist should create a safe and trusting environment where your child feels comfortable expressing their thoughts and emotions. This connection can be pivotal in helping them confront their addiction. As a parent, you can support this by encouraging open dialogue about their feelings toward therapy and the therapist they choose.

Finally, remember that finding the right therapist may take time, and it's okay to seek out multiple consultations before making a decision. Each therapist brings a unique perspective and approach, and it's important to find someone who aligns with your child's needs and values. Trust your instincts as a parent and remain actively involved in this process, remembering that your support is a vital component in your child's recovery journey.

Evaluating Treatment Options

Evaluating treatment options for children struggling with substance abuse is a critical step for parents. It is essential to understand that not all treatment methods are created equal, and what works for one child may not work for another. Parents should start by researching various types of therapies, including behavioral therapies, medication-assisted treatment, and holistic approaches. Each of these options addresses the issue from different angles, and recognizing the unique needs of your child is vital in making the right choice.

Communication plays a pivotal role in this evaluation process. Engaging your child in conversations about their treatment can provide insights into their feelings and preferences. It is important to create an open environment where your child feels safe to express themselves. This dialogue can also help parents gauge their child's readiness for change and willingness to participate in different therapeutic approaches, which can significantly influence the effectiveness of the treatment.

Seeking professional help is another crucial aspect of evaluating treatment options. Parents should consider consulting with healthcare providers who specialize in adolescent substance abuse. These professionals can offer personalized recommendations based on your child's specific situation, including the severity of addiction and any co-occurring mental health issues. Attending support groups for parents can also provide valuable information and shared experiences that can assist in making informed decisions about treatment.

Creating a supportive home environment is equally important when evaluating treatment options. A nurturing atmosphere can enhance the effectiveness of any treatment your child undergoes. Parents should focus on establishing routines, setting clear boundaries, and fostering open communication. This supportive framework not only aids in recovery but also helps children feel secure and understood, which is essential during this challenging time.

Finally, it is crucial for parents to educate themselves continuously about substance abuse and recovery options. Knowledge empowers parents to make informed decisions and advocate for their child's needs. Engaging in family activities that promote healthy habits can also be beneficial. By participating in these activities, families can bond and create positive experiences that counteract the negative influences of addiction, paving the way for a healthier future together.

Finding Support Groups

Finding support groups can be a crucial step for parents dealing with a child's substance abuse. These groups provide a safe space for sharing experiences, learning from others, and gaining valuable insights into coping strategies. Parents often feel isolated and overwhelmed, but connecting with others facing similar challenges can foster a sense of community and understanding. Support groups can vary in size, format, and focus, so it's important to explore options that resonate with your needs and comfort level.

Many communities offer local support groups that meet regularly, allowing parents to share their experiences in person. Organizations like Al-Anon or Nar-Anon specifically cater to families and friends of individuals struggling with addiction. In addition to local groups, online support forums and virtual meetings have become popular, especially for those who may find it difficult to attend in person. These platforms can provide anonymity and convenience, making it easier to reach out for help.

When searching for a support group, consider the specific issues you want to address. Some groups focus on particular substances, while others may discuss broader topics related to addiction and recovery.

Checking the credentials of the group facilitators and the structure of the meetings can also help ensure that you find a supportive environment. It's essential to feel safe and respected within the group, as this will encourage open communication and sharing.

In addition to finding a support group, parents should also seek professional help. Therapists specializing in addiction can offer guidance and coping strategies tailored to your family's unique situation. Many therapists also have connections with support groups, creating a comprehensive approach to recovery that includes both professional and peer support. This dual approach can be especially effective in navigating the complexities of addiction and its impact on family dynamics.

Ultimately, finding support groups is about creating a network of care that empowers you as a parent. It's vital to remember that you are not alone in this journey, and reaching out for help is a sign of strength. By connecting with others, sharing experiences, and learning from one another, you can cultivate resilience and hope as you navigate the challenges of your child's addiction together.

CHAPTER 5

CREATING A SUPPORTIVE

HOME ENVIRONMENT FOR

RECOVERY

Establishing House Rules and Boundaries

Establishing house rules and boundaries is a critical step for parents of children struggling with substance abuse. Clear guidelines help create a structured environment where children can feel safe and understood. Parents should sit down with their child to discuss expectations and consequences, emphasizing the importance of these rules in supporting their recovery journey. This collaborative approach fosters open communication and reinforces the concept that rules are not just punitive but are designed to protect and guide.

In addition to setting rules, it is essential to define specific boundaries regarding substance use. Parents need to be firm yet compassionate in their stance against drug and alcohol use. Discussing the potential impacts of substance abuse, both immediate and long-term, can help children understand the reasoning behind these boundaries. By articulating the risks and consequences associated with substance use, parents can encourage their children to make healthier choices.

Creating a supportive home environment involves more than just rules; it requires consistency and follow-through. Parents must be prepared to enforce the established boundaries while also providing emotional support. Regular family meetings can serve as a platform for discussing any challenges and celebrating successes. This ongoing dialogue helps reinforce the family unit and demonstrates to the child that they are not alone in their struggles.

Lastly, seeking professional help and connecting with support networks can enhance the effectiveness of house rules. Parents should consider involving therapists or support groups that specialize in addiction recovery. These professionals can provide valuable insights and strategies to reinforce the home environment, ensuring that both parents and children have the resources they need to navigate the challenges of addiction together. Building a community of support can alleviate feelings of isolation and empower families to work as a team toward recovery.

Encouraging Open Communication

Encouraging open communication with your child about substance abuse is crucial in navigating their recovery journey. As a parent, it is essential to create an environment where your child feels safe to express their thoughts and feelings without judgment. This openness not only fosters trust but also allows for more honest discussions about the challenges they face and the support they need. By actively listening and validating their experiences, you can help them feel understood and less isolated in their struggles.

One effective strategy is to initiate conversations during relaxed moments, rather than waiting for a crisis. Choose a time when your child is more likely to engage, perhaps during a family meal or while doing an activity together. This approach can make it easier for them to open up about their feelings and experiences with addiction. Remember to use open-ended questions that encourage dialogue, showing genuine interest in their lives and concerns. This will help them feel valued and more willing to share their thoughts.

Additionally, it is important to educate yourself about the nature of addiction and its impact on your child. Understanding the different types of substances and their effects can provide you with the knowledge needed to engage in more informed discussions. This knowledge not only empowers you as a parent but also demonstrates to your child that you are taking their situation seriously. They will appreciate your efforts to understand their challenges and may be more inclined to communicate openly.

Creating a supportive home environment is another vital aspect of encouraging open communication. Establish family rules that promote healthy behaviors and make it clear that your home is a safe space for discussions about addiction. Ensure that your child knows they can talk to you about their struggles without fear of punishment or negative consequences. This kind of environment can significantly reduce feelings of shame and promote honesty in your relationship.

Lastly, consider seeking professional help if communication becomes challenging. Therapists and support groups can provide additional resources and support for both you and your child. Engaging in family therapy can also help improve communication dynamics and foster a better understanding of each other's feelings and perspectives. By taking these steps, you can create a foundation of open communication that can aid in your child's recovery and strengthen your family bond.

Fostering a Positive Atmosphere

Creating a positive atmosphere is essential for the recovery journey of children struggling with substance abuse. As a parent, fostering an environment that encourages open communication, understanding, and support can significantly impact your child's willingness to engage in recovery. By setting the tone at home, you can help your child feel safe and valued, which is crucial in their healing process. This positive atmosphere serves as a foundation for addressing addiction and promoting healthy behaviors.

One effective strategy is to maintain a non-judgmental stance when discussing substance use. Parents should aim to listen more than they speak, allowing their children to express their feelings and struggles without fear of backlash or criticism. This approach not only builds trust but also encourages children to be more open about their challenges. It is important to validate their experiences and emotions, showing that you understand their struggles while guiding them toward healthier choices.

In addition to communication, engaging in family activities that promote healthy habits can reinforce a positive atmosphere. These activities can include cooking healthy meals together, exercising, or participating in hobbies that interest your child. Such shared experiences not only strengthen family bonds but also distract from negative influences and provide alternative coping mechanisms. Creating routines that emphasize health and well-being can help shift the focus away from substance use towards more constructive pursuits.

Seeking professional help is another vital component of fostering a positive atmosphere. Finding therapists and support groups that specialize in addiction can provide both you and your child with valuable resources and coping strategies. These professionals can offer insights into the nature of addiction and recovery, equipping families with the tools needed to navigate this challenging journey. Remember that you are not alone; connecting with other parents in similar situations can also provide support and encouragement.

Lastly, maintaining your mental health is crucial as a parent. Coping with a child's addiction can be emotionally taxing, and prioritizing your well-being enables you to be a more effective support system. Engage in self-care practices, seek therapy for yourself, and lean on your support network to manage stress. By ensuring that you are mentally and emotionally healthy, you create a more stable environment that benefits not only you but also your child as they work towards recovery.

CHAPTER 6

COPING MECHANISMS FOR

PARENTS

Prioritizing Your Mental Health

Prioritizing your mental health as a parent of a child with substance problems is crucial. The stress and emotional toll of dealing with your child's addiction can be overwhelming. It's essential to recognize that taking care of yourself is not selfish but rather a necessary step in supporting your child effectively. By maintaining your mental well-being, you equip yourself with the strength and clarity needed to navigate the challenges ahead.

Understanding different types of addiction in children can help you better comprehend what your child is experiencing. Each type of addiction may require different approaches and responses. Educating yourself about substance abuse will enable you to engage in informed discussions with your child and seek appropriate help. This knowledge can also alleviate some of the fear and confusion that often accompany a loved one's addiction.

Communication plays a vital role in addressing addiction. Developing strategies for talking to your child about their struggles can foster a supportive environment. It's important to approach these conversations with empathy and patience, ensuring your child feels heard and understood. This communication can also pave the way for seeking professional help together, including finding therapists and support groups tailored to both your child's needs and your own.

Lastly, navigating school and social life while addressing addiction requires careful consideration. Encouraging your child to engage with peers and participate in healthy activities can aid their recovery. Building connections with other parents in similar situations can also provide valuable support and understanding, allowing you to share experiences and coping strategies. Prioritizing your mental health not only benefits you but also enhances your ability to support your child through their recovery journey.

Stress Management Techniques

Stress can be an overwhelming part of being a parent to a child struggling with addiction. It is crucial to recognize and implement effective stress management techniques to maintain your mental health and support your child through their recovery journey. Simple practices such as mindfulness, deep breathing exercises, and regular physical activity can significantly reduce stress levels. By prioritizing your well-being, you create a more stable environment for both you and your child, allowing for better communication and support during challenging times.

Establishing a routine can also be immensely beneficial in managing stress. A daily schedule that includes time for self-care, family activities, and open discussions about addiction can foster a sense of normalcy and control. Consistency helps both you and your child understand what to expect, which can alleviate anxiety. Incorporating relaxing activities such as yoga, meditation, or even a daily walk can provide necessary breaks and promote a healthier mindset.

Additionally, seeking support from others can be an effective way to cope with the pressures of parenting a child with addiction. Connecting with other parents in similar situations can provide a sense of community and understanding. Support groups, either in-person or online, can offer valuable insights and coping strategies from those who have faced similar challenges, making you feel less isolated in your struggles.

Communication is key when addressing addiction. Practicing open and honest dialogues with your child about their struggles can not only strengthen your relationship but also help in reducing your own stress. By creating a safe space for conversation, you allow your child to express their feelings and concerns, which can lead to better understanding and mutual support. Remember, it's important to approach these discussions with empathy and patience, as addiction is a complex issue.

Finally, prioritize engaging in family activities that promote healthy habits. Whether it's cooking nutritious meals together, participating in sports, or enjoying hobbies as a family, these activities can serve as a positive outlet for both you and your child. Fostering a supportive home environment that encourages healthy choices will not only aid in your child's recovery but also help you manage stress effectively, ensuring that you both navigate this challenging journey together.

Seeking Personal Therapy

Seeking personal therapy is an essential step for parents who are navigating the challenging journey of their child's substance abuse. Understanding that you are not alone in this situation can provide immense relief. Therapy offers a safe space for parents to express their feelings, fears, and frustrations. It also allows for the exploration of personal coping strategies that can help manage the emotional toll of having a child struggling with addiction.

Finding the right therapist is crucial. Parents should look for professionals who specialize in addiction, particularly those who understand the unique dynamics of family systems affected by substance abuse. Many therapists offer family therapy sessions that include not only the parent but also the child, helping to foster communication and healing within the family unit. It is also beneficial to seek therapists who can provide resources and tools tailored to the specific needs of families dealing with addiction.

Support groups can be another valuable resource for parents. These groups provide an avenue for connecting with others who are experiencing similar challenges. Sharing stories and strategies with fellow parents can alleviate feelings of isolation and provide practical advice. Many organizations and communities offer support groups specifically aimed at parents of children with substance use issues, creating a supportive network that can significantly enhance coping mechanisms.

In addition to individual therapy and support groups, parents should also focus on maintaining their mental health. Engaging in self-care practices, such as exercise, meditation, or hobbies, can help alleviate stress. It is essential for parents to recognize their own emotional needs and take steps to address them. A healthy parent is better equipped to support their child through recovery, making self-care a critical component of the journey.

Creating a supportive home environment is equally important. Parents can reinforce positive habits by establishing routines that promote healthy living and open communication. Engaging in family activities that foster connection and understanding can significantly impact a child's recovery process. By actively participating in their child's recovery journey, parents not only strengthen their relationship but also contribute to a more positive outcome for their child's future.

CHAPTER 7

NAVIGATING SCHOOL AND

SOCIAL LIFE

Communicating with School Officials

Communicating with school officials can be a crucial step in addressing your child's substance abuse issues. It is important to approach these conversations with a clear understanding of your child's situation and the challenges they face. Being informed about the specific substance your child is using can help in articulating concerns effectively. Make sure to gather any relevant documentation, such as grades, attendance records, and behavioral reports, which can provide context to the school officials about your child's struggles.

When you meet with school officials, consider bringing a supportive ally, such as a therapist or a trusted family member, to help facilitate the discussion. This can not only help you feel less isolated but also provide additional perspectives on your child's needs. It is essential to communicate openly about your child's addiction and any related issues, such as mental health concerns or social challenges. This honesty fosters a collaborative approach to finding solutions that can benefit your child's educational experience.

Establishing a positive relationship with school officials is vital for ongoing support. They can become valuable allies in your child's recovery journey, offering resources such as counseling services, academic accommodations, or even referrals to community support groups. Regular follow-ups with teachers and counselors can ensure that everyone is on the same page and can address any emerging issues promptly. This proactive communication also reinforces to your child that their education and well-being are a shared priority.

Educating school officials about addiction can also help reduce stigma and promote a more understanding environment for your child. It is beneficial to share information about substance abuse and its impact on adolescents, as well as the importance of a supportive school culture. Encourage schools to implement training programs for staff to better recognize and respond to students facing addiction, which in turn can create a more empathetic environment for all students.

In conclusion, effective communication with school officials can play a pivotal role in supporting your child's recovery from substance abuse. By approaching these discussions with clarity, openness, and a collaborative spirit, you can help create a network of support that extends beyond the home. This partnership not only aids in your child's academic success but also in their overall healing process, providing them with the tools they need to navigate the challenges of recovery and school life.

Supporting Your Child's Social Needs

Supporting your child's social needs is crucial when navigating the challenges of substance abuse. Children struggling with addiction often face isolation and stigma, which can exacerbate their issues. As a parent, fostering a supportive environment where your child feels safe to express their feelings and concerns is essential. Encourage open dialogue about their experiences and feelings, letting them know they are not alone in this fight. Establishing trust will help them seek your guidance rather than turning to substances as a coping mechanism.

One effective strategy for supporting your child's social needs is to engage them in activities that promote healthy relationships. Encourage participation in group activities, such as team sports or clubs, where they can interact with peers in a positive environment. These activities can help them build a sense of belonging and reduce feelings of isolation. Additionally, consider involving them in community service projects, which can foster empathy and provide a constructive outlet for their energies.

Communication is key when addressing your child's addiction. It is important to approach conversations with empathy and understanding, rather than judgment. Utilize open-ended questions to help them articulate their feelings and experiences. This not only aids in their emotional processing but also reinforces your role as a supportive figure in their life. Be patient, as they may be hesitant to share their struggles initially, but your consistent presence will encourage them to open up over time.

Seeking professional help can also play a pivotal role in supporting your child's recovery. Therapists and support groups can provide valuable resources and coping strategies that you may not have access to as a parent. Encouraging your child to attend these sessions can help them build connections with peers who understand their struggles, making recovery feel less daunting. Additionally, consider joining a support group for parents, as sharing experiences can provide comfort and practical advice.

Creating a supportive home environment is equally important in addressing your child's social needs. Establishing routines that include family meals, game nights, or outdoor activities can strengthen family bonds and create a positive atmosphere. Focus on fostering healthy habits together, such as cooking nutritious meals or exercising. These shared experiences can reinforce your commitment to their recovery journey and help them develop healthier coping mechanisms, ultimately supporting their social needs during this challenging time.

Addressing Peer Pressure

Peer pressure is a significant factor that can influence a child's decision to experiment with substances. It is essential for parents to understand that this pressure can come from friends, social circles, and even media portrayals of substance use. Acknowledging the reality of peer pressure allows parents to engage in meaningful conversations with their children about the risks associated with substance use. By fostering an open dialogue, parents can help their children navigate these social influences more effectively.

One effective strategy for addressing peer pressure is to encourage children to develop strong self-esteem and decision-making skills. Parents can help their children recognize their values and the importance of making choices that align with those values. Role-playing different scenarios can also be beneficial, allowing children to practice how to respond to peer pressure in a safe environment. This preparation can empower them to stand firm in their decisions when faced with challenging situations.

In addition to building self-esteem, parents should be aware of the social environments their children are involved in. Monitoring friendships and social activities can provide insight into potential influences that may lead to substance use. Parents should not only keep an eye on their children's social circles but also encourage positive relationships with peers who promote healthy behaviors. This can create a more supportive network for children as they navigate the complexities of adolescence.

Finally, parents should not hesitate to seek professional help if they feel overwhelmed by the challenges of addressing peer pressure and substance use. Therapists and support groups can offer valuable resources and strategies tailored to each family's unique situation. Connecting with other parents who are facing similar challenges can also provide a sense of community and support, reinforcing that they are not alone in this journey. By addressing peer pressure head-on, parents can help their children make healthier choices and ultimately foster a lasting recovery.

CHAPTER 8

ENGAGING IN FAMILY

ACTIVITIES THAT PROMOTE

HEALTHY HABITS

Creating a Family Routine

Engaging in family activities that promote healthy habits is another effective approach to combating peer pressure. By creating a supportive home environment, parents can help their children feel secure and valued, reducing the likelihood of seeking validation through substance use. Family outings, sports, and hobbies can provide opportunities for bonding and developing a sense of belonging, which is crucial during such formative years.

Creating a family routine is essential for parents navigating the complexities of a child's substance use. Establishing predictable patterns in daily life can provide a sense of stability and security for both parents and children. Regular family meals, scheduled activities, and set times for homework or relaxation can help foster an environment conducive to open communication and recovery. These routines not only benefit the child but also strengthen family bonds, creating a supportive atmosphere where healthy habits can flourish.

Finally, seeking professional help should be integrated into the family routine. Regular therapy sessions or support group meetings for both parents and children can provide essential tools and resources for managing addiction. Making these appointments a part of the family's schedule not only emphasizes their importance but also normalizes the process of seeking help. This collective approach promotes healing and recovery, ensuring that the family can navigate the challenges of addiction together.

Incorporating positive activities into the family routine is vital. Engaging in exercise, family game nights, or cooking together can promote healthy habits and create a distraction from substance use temptations.

These shared experiences encourage connection and reinforce the importance of sobriety in a fun and supportive way. Parents can take this opportunity to model healthy coping mechanisms, showing their children how to manage stress and emotions without turning to substances.

Additionally, maintaining flexibility within the routine is important. While consistency is key, parents should also be prepared to adapt their plans as needed, especially in response to their child's recovery progress. This adaptability demonstrates to children that their needs are a priority, fostering a sense of trust and understanding. Being responsive to their child's emotional state can help prevent potential relapses and reinforce their commitment to sobriety.

Clear communication is another cornerstone of a successful family routine. Setting aside time for family meetings, where everyone can express their feelings and concerns, can help address the challenges surrounding addiction. This open dialogue ensures that children feel heard and understood, making them more likely to share their struggles with substance use. Parents should encourage honesty and support, emphasizing that the family is united in their journey toward recovery.

Finally, seeking professional help should be integrated into the family routine. Regular therapy sessions or support group meetings for both parents and children can provide essential tools and resources for managing addiction. Making these appointments a part of the family's schedule not only emphasizes their importance but also normalizes the process of seeking help. This collective approach promotes healing and recovery, ensuring that the family can navigate the challenges of addiction together.

Exploring New Hobbies Together

Exploring new hobbies together can be an invaluable way for parents and children to reconnect and find joy amidst the challenges of addiction. Engaging in activities that both parties enjoy fosters communication and builds trust, which is crucial during recovery. Whether it's painting, hiking, or even cooking, these shared experiences can help create a positive environment that encourages openness and healing.

Hobbies have the potential to provide a healthy distraction from the stresses associated with addiction. They can also instill a sense of accomplishment and self-worth in children. By participating in activities that promote skill development, children can replace negative habits with positive ones, thereby reinforcing their commitment to recovery. For parents, witnessing their child's growth in these areas can be both uplifting and motivating.

When exploring new hobbies, it's essential to choose activities that cater to the interests of your child. This not only makes the experience enjoyable but also empowers them to take the lead in their recovery journey. Parents should be open to trying new things, even if they are outside their comfort zones. The willingness to embrace new experiences together sets a strong example of resilience and adaptability.

Family activities that promote healthy habits can also serve as a foundation for establishing routines. Consistency in engaging in these hobbies can create a sense of stability, which is often needed in recovery. Additionally, these routines can help mitigate feelings of uncertainty and anxiety, allowing families to navigate the complexities of addiction together in a supportive manner.

Finally, it's important to foster an environment where all family members feel comfortable expressing their thoughts and feelings. Open discussions about hobbies and how they impact recovery can strengthen family bonds. Ultimately, exploring new hobbies together not only aids in the healing process but also reinforces the idea that recovery is a shared journey that can bring families closer than ever before.

Prioritizing Physical Health

Prioritizing physical health is crucial for both parents and children dealing with addiction. For parents, maintaining their own health is essential, as it enables them to better support their children through difficult times. Engaging in regular physical activities, such as walking, yoga, or joining a fitness class, can serve as a powerful coping mechanism. This not only alleviates stress but also sets a positive example for children, demonstrating the importance of self-care.

Creating a supportive home environment also involves promoting healthy habits within the family. Parents can encourage their children to participate in physical activities together, such as biking, hiking, or playing sports. These shared experiences foster bonding and provide an opportunity for open conversations about addiction in a non-threatening setting. It is important for parents to recognize that physical health is intertwined with emotional well-being, creating a holistic approach to recovery.

Healthy eating is another vital aspect of prioritizing physical health. A balanced diet rich in nutrients can enhance mood and energy levels, which are often affected by substance use. Parents should strive to provide nutritious meals and involve their children in meal preparation, turning it into a fun family activity. This not only encourages healthier eating habits but also allows for quality time together, reinforcing family ties.

In addition to physical activity and nutrition, ensuring adequate sleep is essential for both parents and children. Sleep plays a critical role in mental health, and promoting good sleep hygiene can significantly impact recovery efforts. Establishing a consistent bedtime routine, creating a calm sleeping environment, and limiting screen time before bed are effective strategies. Parents should model these behaviors and encourage their children to prioritize sleep as part of their overall health regimen.

Lastly, it is important for parents to seek professional help when needed. Engaging with therapists and support groups can provide parents with the tools to navigate the complexities of addiction. These resources can guide families in developing a comprehensive plan that includes physical health considerations. By prioritizing physical health, parents not only enhance their own well-being but also create a stronger support system for their children as they work toward recovery.

CHAPTER 9

EDUCATING YOURSELF ABOUT

SUBSTANCE ABUSE

Understanding the Science of Addiction

Understanding addiction requires a deep dive into the psychological and physiological aspects of substance use. For parents, grasping these concepts is crucial, as it can illuminate the struggles their children face.

Addiction is not merely a choice; it involves changes in brain chemistry that create a compelling drive to seek substances despite negative consequences. This understanding can help parents approach their child's situation with empathy rather than frustration, paving the way for more effective communication.

Clear communication is another cornerstone of a successful family routine. Setting aside time for family meetings, where everyone can express their feelings and concerns, can help address the challenges surrounding addiction. This open dialogue ensures that children feel heard and understood, making them more likely to share their struggles with substance use. Parents should encourage honesty and support, emphasizing that the family is united in their journey toward recovery.

Different types of addiction manifest in various forms, including alcohol, drugs, and behavioral addictions like gaming or social media. Each type presents unique challenges and may require tailored strategies for intervention and support. Recognizing these distinctions can empower parents to better understand their child's specific struggles and the underlying motivations for their behavior. This knowledge can also assist in identifying the most effective resources for treatment and support.

Effective communication is essential when addressing addiction. Parents must create a safe space where their children feel comfortable discussing their feelings and experiences. Techniques such as active listening, expressing unconditional love, and avoiding judgment can foster open dialogue. This approach not only helps in understanding the child's perspective but also reinforces the bond between parent and child, which is vital for effective recovery.

Seeking professional help is often a necessary step in addressing addiction. Parents should be proactive in finding therapists, support groups, and rehabilitation programs that specialize in adolescent substance abuse. These professionals can provide invaluable resources and guidance tailored to the family's needs. Additionally, engaging with support groups allows parents to connect with others navigating similar challenges, fostering a sense of community and shared experience.

Creating a supportive home environment plays a pivotal role in recovery. Parents can implement routines that promote healthy habits, engage in family activities that encourage bonding, and maintain open lines of communication. By prioritizing mental health and wellness, parents not only support their child's recovery but also bolster their own emotional resilience. This holistic approach fosters a nurturing atmosphere where both parents and children can thrive despite the challenges of addiction.

Learning About Treatment Options

Understanding the various treatment options available for children struggling with substance abuse is crucial for parents. This knowledge equips you to make informed decisions about your child's recovery journey. Treatment options can vary widely, ranging from outpatient therapies to residential programs, each tailored to meet the specific needs of the child. As a parent, familiarizing yourself with these options will help you advocate for your child's best interests and facilitate their path to recovery.

One of the first steps in learning about treatment options is understanding the different types of addiction your child may be facing. Substance abuse can manifest in various forms, including alcohol, prescription drugs, and illicit substances. Each type of addiction may require a different approach to treatment. By educating yourself about these distinctions, you can better assess the appropriate interventions and support systems needed for your child.

Communication is vital when addressing your child's addiction. Developing strategies to talk openly and honestly about their struggles can foster a supportive environment. This includes expressing your concerns without judgment and encouraging your child to share their feelings. Effective communication can help dismantle feelings of shame and isolation, making your child more receptive to seeking help and considering treatment options.

In addition to direct communication, seeking professional help is an essential component of addressing substance abuse.

Finding therapists, counselors, or support groups that specialize in adolescent addiction can provide invaluable resources for both you and your child. These professionals can offer tailored guidance and coping strategies that align with your family's specific situation, making the recovery process more manageable and effective.

Creating a supportive home environment is imperative for your child's recovery. This includes establishing routines, setting clear boundaries, and engaging in family activities that promote healthy habits. By fostering a nurturing atmosphere, you can help your child feel safe and understood, which can significantly enhance their willingness to embrace treatment options. Remember, recovery is a journey that requires patience and involvement from the entire family.

Staying Informed on Current Research

Staying informed on current research regarding substance abuse is crucial for parents navigating the challenges of their child's addiction. Knowledge about the latest studies, treatment options, and recovery strategies empowers parents to make informed decisions and support their children effectively. Regularly seeking out reputable sources such as academic journals, health organizations, and community resources can provide vital insights into the ever-evolving landscape of addiction treatment.

Understanding different types of addiction that may affect children is essential for recognizing specific behaviors and symptoms. Research highlights that addiction can manifest in various forms, including substance use, behavioral addictions, and co-occurring mental health disorders. By familiarizing themselves with these distinctions, parents can better identify their child's struggles and seek appropriate help tailored to their unique situation.

Effective communication is key when discussing addiction with a child. Current research emphasizes the importance of open, honest dialogues that foster trust and understanding. Parents should approach these conversations with empathy, using language that resonates with their child's experiences while avoiding judgment. This supportive communication strategy can significantly impact a child's willingness to engage in recovery efforts and seek help when needed.

Finding professional help is another critical aspect of staying informed. Parents should be aware of the various resources available, including therapists, support groups, and rehabilitation centers. Research indicates that early intervention and tailored treatment plans can lead to more successful recovery outcomes. By actively seeking these resources, parents can ensure their child receives the support necessary for overcoming addiction.

Creating a supportive home environment is essential for recovery. Research shows that a nurturing and understanding atmosphere can significantly influence a child's journey toward sobriety. Parents can promote healthy habits by engaging in family activities that encourage positive interactions and foster a sense of belonging. Additionally, maintaining their mental health is vital for parents, as it allows them to be more effective advocates for their child's recovery and well-being.

CHAPTER 10

BUILDING A SUPPORT

NETWORK

Finding Community Resources

Finding community resources is an essential step for parents navigating the challenges of a child's substance abuse. Local organizations, support groups, and educational programs can provide invaluable assistance and guidance. Parents should start by researching nearby facilities that specialize in addiction treatment and recovery. Many communities have resources tailored specifically for families, offering workshops and information sessions to help parents understand the complexities of addiction.

Support groups, such as Al-Anon or Nar-Anon, can be particularly beneficial for parents seeking comfort and understanding from those who share similar experiences. These groups provide a safe space to discuss feelings, share coping strategies, and learn from others' journeys. Networking with other parents can not only alleviate feelings of isolation but also foster a sense of community that is crucial during difficult times.

In addition to support groups, finding therapists who specialize in adolescent substance abuse can be a game-changer. Professional help can offer tailored strategies for addressing addiction within the family dynamic. Many therapists also provide resources for communication techniques, helping parents engage in constructive conversations with their children about their struggles and needs.

Creating a supportive home environment is vital for recovery. Parents can find resources that help them develop a nurturing atmosphere, focusing on open communication, healthy routines, and family activities that promote wellness. Engaging in these activities together can strengthen family bonds and provide children with a sense of security and belonging, which is crucial during recovery.

Lastly, educating oneself about substance abuse and treatment options is key to effectively supporting a child in recovery. Parents can access numerous online resources, books, and community programs that deepen their understanding of addiction. By staying informed, parents can advocate for their child's needs and actively participate in their recovery journey, ensuring they are not alone in this challenging process.

Connecting with Other Parents

Connecting with other parents who are facing similar challenges is crucial for those navigating the difficult landscape of their child's substance abuse issues. Sharing experiences can provide not only valuable insights but also emotional support. Building a network of understanding peers allows parents to feel less isolated in their struggles, knowing that they are not alone in their journey. This connection can foster a sense of community, where members uplift each other and share coping strategies that have worked in their own families.

Effective communication is key when engaging with other parents. It's important to create an open and non- judgmental environment where feelings and experiences can be freely exchanged. Parents should feel encouraged to discuss their fears, successes, and the various challenges they face while coping with their children's addiction. This dialogue can lead to discovering new perspectives and approaches that may be beneficial, as well as reinforcing the notion that it's okay to seek help.

Participating in support groups specifically designed for parents can be immensely beneficial. These groups often provide structured environments where parents can share their stories and receive guidance from professionals. Additionally, many support groups offer resources and referrals to therapists and treatment options, which can be invaluable for parents trying to find the right help for their children. The shared experiences within these groups can also serve as a reminder of the importance of self-care and maintaining one's mental health.

Family activities that encourage healthy habits can also be a great way to connect with other parents. Organizing group outings, such as hiking, cooking classes, or wellness workshops, can strengthen bonds among families while promoting a positive environment for recovery. Engaging in these activities together not only fosters friendships but also reinforces the idea that recovery and healthy living can be a shared journey rather than an individual struggle.

Ultimately, creating a supportive home environment is vital for both the child and the parents. By connecting with other parents, individuals can learn to create spaces filled with understanding, love, and encouragement. These connections can lead to more resilient family dynamics, where everyone feels empowered to contribute to the recovery process. Building a network of support and understanding is an essential step in navigating the complexities of addiction within the family.

Utilizing Online Support Groups

In today's digital age, online support groups have emerged as invaluable resources for parents navigating the tumultuous waters of their children's substance abuse issues. These platforms provide a space where parents can share their experiences, seek advice, and find comfort in knowing they are not alone. By participating in these groups, parents can connect with others who understand the unique challenges they face, fostering a sense of community that is often hard to find in their immediate surroundings.

Engaging with online support groups allows parents to educate themselves about different types of addiction and the various treatment options available. Many groups feature members who have firsthand experience with addiction, offering insights that can be both enlightening and practical. This knowledge can empower parents to approach their child's situation with a more informed perspective, enabling them to ask the right questions and make better decisions regarding professional help and interventions.

Communication is crucial when addressing substance abuse, and online support groups often provide strategies for effectively talking to children about their addiction. Parents can learn from the experiences of others who have successfully navigated these difficult conversations, gaining tips on how to foster an open dialogue without judgment. This exchange of ideas can help create a more supportive environment at home, where children feel safe discussing their struggles and seeking help.

In addition to support and information, online groups can also serve as an emotional outlet for parents. The stress and anxiety that accompany a child's addiction can be overwhelming, and having a space to express these feelings is essential for maintaining mental health. Sharing personal stories and coping mechanisms with others who truly understand can alleviate feelings of isolation, providing parents with the resilience needed to support their children.

Finally, online support groups can facilitate connections with local resources, such as therapists and community programs. Many parents find it helpful to share recommendations and experiences regarding professional help, which can lead to finding the right support for their family. By utilizing these online platforms, parents can build a robust support network that not only aids their children's recovery but also enhances their own coping strategies and overall well-being.

STAY IN THE KNOW,

EDUCATING YOURSELF ON

In "Knowledge is Power," discover essential strategies for educating yourself about substance abuse and recovery options for your child. This comprehensive guide emphasizes the importance of open communication, creating a supportive home environment, and connecting with professional help and peer support. Empower yourself with knowledge to navigate the challenging journey of addiction and recovery, fostering resilience and hope for your family.

www.ingramcontent.com/pod-product-compliance
Lightning Source LLC
Chambersburg PA
CBHW051928220626
47052CB00003B/619